Jack and the beanstalk

written by HY MURDOCK
illustrated by LYNN N GRUNDY

Ladybird Books Loughborough

Once upon a time there was a little boy called Jack who lived with his mother. They were very poor and one day, when there was no money left to buy food, they had to sell their cow. Jack went off to market and on the way he met a farmer.

This well-known fairytale is delightfully illustrated
and simply retold to entertain all young listeners.

Titles in Series S852
Cinderella
Three Little Pigs
Goldilocks and the Three Bears
Jack and the beanstalk
Snow White and the Seven Dwarfs
These titles are also available as a Gift Box set

British Library Cataloguing in Publication Data
Murdock, Hy
    Jack and the beanstalk. — (Fairy tales. Series 852; 4)
    I. Title   II. Grundy, Lynn N.   III. Series
    823'.914[J]   PZ8
    ISBN 0-7214-9529-X

First Edition

© LADYBIRD BOOKS LTD MCMLXXXV
© Illustrations LYNN N GRUNDY MCMLXXXV
All rights reserved. No part of this publication may be reproduced, stored in a retrieval
system, or transmitted in any form or by any means, electronic, mechanical, photo-copying,
recording or otherwise, without the prior consent of the copyright owners.

"I'll buy your cow for these magic beans," said the farmer. Jack was very excited and he sold the cow. Then he ran all the way home to show the beans to his mother.

But Jack's mother was very angry. She sent him to bed without any supper and she threw the magic beans out of the window.

Next morning, when Jack looked out of the window, he couldn't believe his eyes. There was the biggest beanstalk he had ever seen! It grew up and up and up, right through the clouds. "Those beans really *were* magic," thought Jack. "I wonder what's at the top?"

And so, before his mother was awake, he set off to climb to the top of the beanstalk.

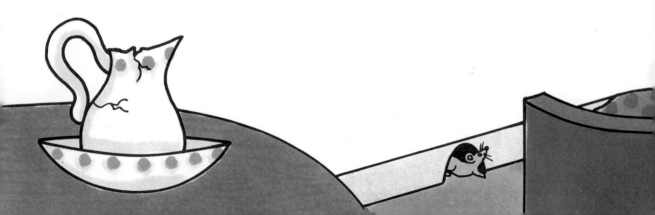

At the top Jack saw an enormous castle. Jack was very hungry after his long climb so he decided to knock on the castle door and ask for some food.

The door was opened by a huge woman. She felt sorry for Jack and asked him to come inside. She gave him some bread and cheese but she told Jack to be careful. Her husband was a giant and he liked to eat little boys.

But then the castle began to shake. It was the giant coming! "Quick!" said the woman to Jack. "Hide in here," and she pushed him into the oven. The giant sniffed and roared,
  "Fee-fi-fo-fum,
    I smell the blood of an Englishman!"
"There's no one here," said his wife. "You sit down and eat your breakfast."

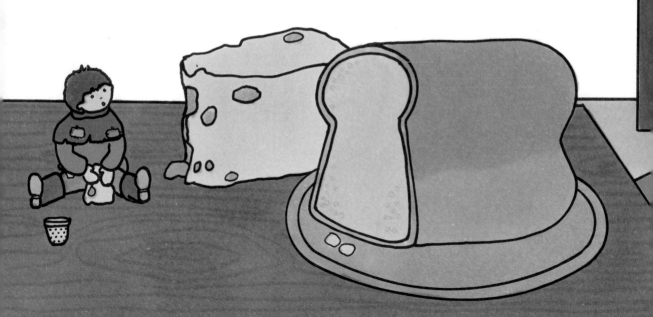

After he had eaten, the giant took out some bags of gold and started to count his money. Soon he fell asleep and began to snore. Jack crept out of the oven and went to the table. He picked up a bag of gold and away he ran.

He climbed back down the beanstalk as fast as he could and rushed into the house to show the gold to his mother.

For a time Jack and his mother lived happily
until they had spent all the gold. Then Jack
decided that he would have to go back to
the giant's castle. Early one morning he
climbed up the beanstalk again.

Jack knocked on the castle door. This time the woman was not so friendly because she knew that it was Jack who had taken a bag of gold. In the end she did let him in and she gave him some breakfast.

Then everything happened just as before. Jack hid in the oven. The giant came in roaring, *"Fee-fi-fo-fum."* But his wife made him sit down to eat his breakfast.

Afterwards the giant said, "Bring me the hen that lays the golden eggs." Jack peeped out. The giant stroked the hen and said, "Lay!" and it laid a golden egg.

After a while the giant felt sleepy and soon he was snoring loudly. Jack jumped out of the oven, picked up the hen and rushed back down the beanstalk as fast as he could go.

Jack showed his mother what the hen could do and soon they were very rich.

Jack did not need to go back up the beanstalk but he liked adventures. So one morning off he went again. This time he didn't knock on the castle door. He waited for a chance to creep inside and he hid in the big tub where the woman washed the clothes.

Soon the giant and his wife came in. The giant sniffed and roared,
   "Fee-fi-fo-fum,
   I smell the blood of an Englishman!"

The woman said, "If it's that boy who stole your gold and the hen, he'll be hiding in the oven." But Jack wasn't in the oven.

After breakfast, the giant asked for his golden harp. It was a magic harp. When the giant said, ''Sing,'' it played beautiful music. Soon the giant was asleep again. Jack came out from his hiding place. He picked up the harp and ran out of the castle.

But as he ran, the magic harp shouted, ''Master! Master!'' The giant woke up and chased after Jack. Jack was puffing by the time he reached the beanstalk. He climbed down but the giant was still chasing him.

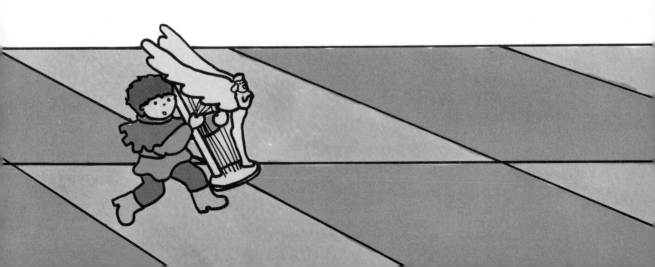

Down, down, down went Jack and down came the giant after him.

As he got to the bottom, Jack shouted to his mother, "Bring me an axe!" Jack chopped and chopped until the beanstalk began to fall. Just in time it crashed to the ground and so did the giant. And that was the end of him.

Jack had had enough adventures by now and so he and his mother lived happily ever after.